RAISING THE ROYAL BARRE

RONARIA'S PRINCES

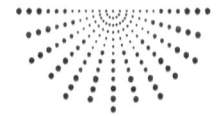

CONSTANCE PHILLIPS

Edited by
GILLY WRIGHT
Cover art by
PAGE AND SAGE

CONSTANCE PHILLIPS PRESS

For those who ignore where the bar is set and shoot to exceed all expectations.

CHAPTER ONE

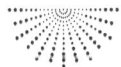

$\mathcal{I}$ took the tray from Georgianne and held it as she moved her now-famous lemon tarts to the display case. My boisterous and chatty boss had been uncharacteristically quiet this morning, and I couldn't help but worry.

I knew she was no different than the rest of us—even if she was now engaged to Ronaria's Prince Layton—but her sullen mood sent a wave of nausea through my stomach.

Something wasn't right.

When Georgianne opened *Viviana's Bistro* a couple of years ago, sales had been unstable. She'd obsessed over the business she'd named in honor of her late mother, over the daily receipts and expenditures, to the point I feared for my job.

I knew she was as loyal to me as I was to her. We were, after all, sisters, in a not-by-blood sort of way. You see, her father served as a top administrator at the orphanage I'd grown up in. I might have been a child of the system, never finding a home of my own after being removed from my mother's care at the age of nine, but James Bosco and his wife, Viviana, had provided temporary respite on the occasions I found myself between arrangements stamped *permanent foster situations*.

The longest lasted six months.

The feelings of being lost and abandoned had cultivated a need in me. One I finally felt mature and stable enough to pursue. I wanted to provide a safe and loving home to an older child—one like me—who was less likely to find a family to call their own otherwise.

Not like my own mother who chose drugs, alcohol, and revolving men over me. Not like the too-numerous-to-count foster families whose love I learned was conditional on my behavior.

Not for brief spans of time. Forever.

The way a parent was supposed to love a child.

James and Viviana were the closest thing to parents I'd ever known, and Georgianne had been a loving and supportive big sister—protecting me when necessary—most often from myself.

Before I'd been removed from my mother's home, I'd been the type of child who worked so hard to please others, believing if I could make Mom happy she would love me enough. After the official children's services came, my attitude spun one-hundred-eighty degrees. I rebelled, pushed boundaries, and acted out to build walls and prove the misguided notion I was unlovable.

The only ones who didn't react as I expected—and send me back into the system—were the Boscos. Instead they would take me in until James's team could find another placement for me. He never gave up on me or the idea I could be reached and helped.

When I aged out of the system and needed a job, Georgianne didn't hesitate to hire me. It didn't matter her budget didn't allow for an employee, she found a way to keep me on.

No one was happier than me was when she found her literal Prince Charming.

Ronaria's Prince Layton—in town for Queen Margaret's child welfare summit—had walked into the bistro and swept Georgianne off her feet.

The two were from different worlds, but they had proved love could win out when each partner was willing to work at it. Both made allowance and sacrifices so they could be together.

Because Layton was the sixth-in-line—and not likely to take the throne—he'd been able to move to Montgomery so Georgianne could keep the coffee shop and be near her father.

Ever since, business had grown steadily. I'd even heard the couple discussing a second location in recent weeks, which was why Georgianne's mood puzzled me.

One thing I knew for sure, good things never last. If Georgianne was worried, there was cause to be. Not knowing how to broach the subject, I reached for a colloquial doorway. "Penny for your thoughts."

Georgianne's attention snapped to me, and she forced a smile. "It's obvious that I'm preoccupied. Isn't it?"

"A little."

"Quinton is arriving today for a visit."

My mouth went dry and I swallowed hard. Before I'd ever heard of Layton Kotnic, Prince of Ronaria, I'd known of—idolized—Prince Quinton Kotnic, ballet dancer. Though I was never *really* good at it, Viviana enrolled me in dance classes when I lived with them, and I'd fallen in love, searching the internet for videos of performances.

In one performance from the National Slovakian Ballet company Quinton had danced as guest principal.

He'd seemed to drop off the world stage a few years ago, and I'd wondered what happened, I'd often thought of asking

Layton about his brother, but never wanted to breech his sense of privacy when it came to his family. "Layton's brother?"

"The next oldest, the one he's closest to."

"Layton must be excited to see him."

"He is. We're both worried he's delivering a plea for us to return to Ronaria."

Layton had devoted his life to children's welfare before deciding to relocate to Montgomery. Nothing had changed since—he first worked in our country's child welfare departments and later took a position in our queen's charitable foundation. Both positions enhanced his likability on the world stage. It seemed everyone admired him for his humanitarian efforts and extreme modesty. Layton didn't thrive in the spotlight like Quinton once had; in fact, he avoided it as much as possible.

I suppose that's why he seemed blissfully happy in his new life. Until this moment, I believed Layton had the full support of his royal siblings and parents. "Why would the family want him home, if that's not where he wants to be?"

"We don't know for sure that is the reason for his visit. The guise seems to be to bring us a housewarming gift, but I can't help but worry. I can tell Layton is nervous too."

If Quinton persuaded Layton to return to Ronaria, there was no question Georgianne would follow. A year ago, my boss might have chosen her business over romance, but these twelve months of Layton's love had molded her. She would follow him around the globe.

Georgianne took the empty tray from my hands. "I'm going to put this away and make a few calls. Sitting here waiting for Quinton to arrive will only drive me crazy."

I felt my knees nearly buckle. "He's coming here?"

"Queen Margaret is sending a car as a favor to Layton. We'll all meet up here."

"If it helps, I can finish the prep work and open the doors."

Georgianne touched my shoulder. "I have full faith in you, Isabel. The other girls will be here shortly. Turn on the lights, set the register, and open the doors as soon as all of you are ready."

I picked up the frilly white apron from under the counter and tied it in place. I'd been skeptical of the new uniforms Layton suggested six months ago. I was sure the black pencil skirt and black dress shirt would show every speck of flour and sugar and the white frills of the apron would be easily caught and torn, but they'd proven to be durable. I'd even grown fond of the higher-end look they gave the shop.

Today, I was grateful for the neat, clean appearance, and ran my fingers over my hair hoping it was all tucked neatly into my ponytail. I'd never imagined I ever see Quinton Kotnic in person, let alone have the chance to speak with him.

Jana and Lenore filed in from the back just as I finished setting the register for the day, so I crossed the room and flipped the switch that lit up the sign and windows.

As I twisted the lock, I noticed the man who I'd watched dance on my computer screen countless times climb out of a black sedan bearing the emblem of the Royal Family of Montgomery on the door. For the first time, I noticed the striking similarity between him and his brother, yet the differences were just as obvious. Quinton was a longer, leaner version of his sibling. Where Layton's posture and stance could only be described as royal, Quinton carried himself in a way exuding strength and poise.

As the man approached, I held the door. I'd like to say I remembered everything I'd been taught about properly respecting a member of a royal family when I curtseyed, but

5

it was more because my nerves got the best of me. "You must be Prince Quinton of Ronaria."

He touched my arm and held my gaze. My flesh warmed beneath his hand. "Please. There is no need for formalities."

I let go of the door, letting it glide shut. His green eyes held an intensity I'd never seen. Though he smiled warmly, he looked weighted down by something. I couldn't help but wonder if Georgianne was spot-on with her concerns.

Even though his presence might inevitably cost me my job a tingle still crawled my spine and my stomach fluttered when our eyes met.

Not knowing what to say, I simply nodded.

He looked to the nametag on my shoulder. "Isabel. Lovely name for a beautiful woman."

A smooth talker, this one. I called out to Jana. "Would you tell Georgianne Prince Quinton is here?"

"What did I tell you about formalities?"

Though he seemed to protest the title—much like Layton did—Quinton's modesty rang false. He walked past me, and I rounded the counter, trying my best to make a good impression on Georgianne's behalf. "Would you like something? A cup of coffee?"

"A double shot of espresso would be wonderful. It was a dreadfully long trip."

I picked up a cup and placed it on the tray on the large stainless-steel machine. Working my way through the steps, I steeled myself. Just being in the same room with the object of my dance obsession made my head spin, and I fought the desire to turn back and soak in the man's muscular frame and good looks.

Don't forget he's here to convince Layton to go home, which in turn would close this shop and cost me my job.

Once I had the brewing process started, I turned back to the counter and picked up a plate and the tongs. I opened the case and placed an assortment of our most popular treats on the plate: a lemon tart, an apple blossom, a cannoli, and a chocolate cookie." I carried the plate around the counter and motioned for Quinton to follow me. "You and Georgianne can sit over here. She will be right out, and I'll bring you your espresso as soon as it's ready."

He paused in front of the table, his stare causing my body to flush. "Thank you for your hospitality, but I don't have the same sweet tooth my brother does."

"Really?" I motioned to the cookie. "Who doesn't like chocolate?"

Georgianne approached. "Quinton doesn't. Can you bring me a cup of coffee and a blueberry scone for him?"

"That would be nice," he responded and then opened his arms to Georgianne. "It is so good to see you."

I noticed she wavered before stepping into his embrace. Her hesitance clicked off a warning alarm. Was Georgianne really worried about Quinton's visit, or had she not been as warmly accepted by the royal family of Ronaria as I once believed?

Still a lick of jealousy settled low in my stomach as Quinton closed the embrace. I quickly shook it off, turning back to the counter to fulfill Georgianne's request.

At the counter, I placed the scone on a plate and filled a cup with coffee as I watched Quinton step back while keeping his hands on Georgianne's shoulders.

His entire focus seemed to be on his soon-to-be sister-in-law; I couldn't take my eyes off him.

I picked up the plate and mug, set to go back to the table, when Jana interrupted my train of thought. "Can you tell Georgianne Layton is on the phone?"

"Certainly." As I approached the table again, Quinton said, "Mother ordered me to inquire on the date for the nuptials."

7

Georgianne twisted her hands. "Your brother and I have narrowed it down to early fall."

"Of this year?" Quinton laughed. "Do you know how long it takes to plan a royal affair?"

Georgianne shrugged. "Have you met your brother? He's insisting on as low-key wedding as possible."

I set the plate on the table in front of Quinton and the mug in front of Georgianne. "Layton is on the phone for you."

She slipped from the booth. "Can you sit and keep Quinton company?"

He didn't look like the type who needed to be monitored. I wondered if Georgianne was adhering to some sort of royal protocol I wasn't aware of. She'd grown quite comfortable with all the etiquette between her interactions with Montgomery's and Ronaria's royal families, I would take her lead and trust her guidance, even though I was sure my nerves would cause me to misspeak and say something stupid. I slid into the booth and found myself lost in the prince's bright green eyes.

He watched Georgianne disappear through the door to the kitchen. "She keeps herself very busy."

"It's her bistro. She's always been very hands on."

He smirked and broke off a piece of the scone with a fork. "And that's why Georgianne is a perfect match for Layton. She shies away from the limelight almost as much as he does."

Modesty *was* a suit Layton wore well, and it was a trait I adored about him. I always imagined his humility came from the way he was raised. Meeting Quinton now, I wondered if my assessment was true.

"Just like with this wedding," he continued. "Where does he get the idea they can have something simple and private?"

"From what Georgianne tells me, neither wants money

spent on a ceremony that could be used to help the people of Ronaria."

"Neither my parents nor their subjects will allow their wedding to be anything but a stunning event." Quinton broke off another piece of the scone. After chewing thoroughly and swallowing, he said. "It might take some time, but Georgianne will come to learn what it means to be royal and what her and my brother's marriage means to our country."

My stomach twisted into tighter knots. The way he spoke, Georgianne's worse fears seemed to be coming true. I wanted to be sympathetic to what this would mean for the woman I'd come to think of as my sister, but I was preoccupied by how this would affect me and my plans to adopt.

If Layton returned to Ronaria once they were married, Georgianne would have to either sell or close the restaurant. Without a job, not only would I have to put my immediate plans on hold, but my ability to pay my rent would be called into question.

If I were to continue entertaining Quinton, maybe it would be best for my sanity if I changed the subject. "Georgianne mentioned you head up Ronaria's art council."

He nodded. "I do. It's not really all that interesting to be honest. I'm sure you would enjoy talking to my two oldest brothers more. They are more like Layton."

It seemed he was trying to downplay his role in his family's rule of their small nation. At first, Quinton seemed standoffish, now I wondered if was just uncomfortable in the unfamiliar surroundings. It hadn't been *that* long since he'd stepped away from dancing. "I try to follow politics and be informed about the world around me, but honestly, I'm much more interested in dancing and the arts. I find it sad some countries are cutting the arts out of their public schools."

He stiffened. "Did Georgianne tell you about my former life?"

I pulled my lower lip between my teeth, wondering if I should admit my admiration. Honesty quickly won out. "She didn't have to. I'm a longtime fan of your work."

His shoulders relaxed, and he eased back into his seat, reaching into his suit jacket. For the first time since he came into the restaurant, his smile seemed genuine, pushing up his cheeks and lighting up his eyes. "It's wonderful to meet someone who has an appreciation."

Pulling out his phone, he woke it up and clicked at the screen a few times, before turning it toward me. "I was in Slovakia a few weeks ago visiting with my friends from their national ballet. There, I found these pieces done by a local artist. There are four pictures. Slide left."

I thumbed through the pictures of snowy landscapes done with such bright colors and crisp lines I could feel the arctic chill the artist tried to convey. "These are beautiful."

"I hope Layton likes them. They are a housewarming gift for Georgianne and him."

"I'm sure he will love them."

"My hope is they remind him of home."

Fear pinged through me again. The only reason to remind Layton of home would be to encourage him to return. I pushed back against my desire to outright ask if he was on a mission to stir up my life. "I'm ashamed to admit I knew very little about Ronaria until we met Layton. I do know Slovakia is a close neighbor. The landscape must be similar?"

"Don't be ashamed, we are but a blip on the map. The rest of the world finds it easy to ignore us." His hand brushed against mine sending an electrical charge through me.

I tried to ignore my need to be touched by him again and returned his phone. "From the way Layton speaks, it sounds like a lovely country. He talks about the philanthropic work you and all your brothers do. You should be proud."

He visibly cringed. "Layton works hard to make the world a better place. My role seems to be fundraising for the sake of art and culture."

"It can be a cruel world, we need all the beauty we can get."

His gaze bore through me. He seemed to be contemplating my words, considering me. I felt exposed under his stare. Could he read my thoughts? Could he tell how attracted I was to him? Something out of the corner of his eye caught his attention, and he slid out of the booth, standing.

I started to rise, but Georgianne came into my line of sight, waving for us to stay seated. "Layton is dealing with a crisis. He hopes to be here soon."

"They couldn't even give me the chance to talk to Layton myself. Who called? Was it Brodrick or Adrian?"

Georgianne tipped her head. "Why would your brothers be calling about the earthquake in Italy that leveled an orphanage?"

Quinton looked as though he wanted to kick himself. He fidgeted with his jacket, trying to flatten wrinkles that weren't there. "Because they know Layton would be concerned."

Quinton's response slid by me, all I could focus on was the tragedy Georgianne had mentioned. "Oh no! Leveled? Were there any casualties?"

Georgianne's eyes drifted closed. Her horror was evident on her face. "It's only happened within the hour. There are three missing, and six children injured. The rest are accounted for and shaken up but fine." Georgianne turned her attention to Quinton, laying her hand on his shoulder. "Details of the earthquake haven't hit the news yet. You thought your brothers called about something else. Layton and I are excited that you're here, but I *am* confused. Is there more to this? Is there something going on in Ronaria we should know about?"

He gave a curt nod. "I would prefer to discuss it with both of you at once. How much longer will he be?"

"A half hour is what he hoped. They were just getting some first reports, and he and our queen wanted to set a team to start organizing the initial responses. As soon as they have a plan of action, he will be able to take a break."

With the turn in the conversation, I felt like an outsider looking in on a family meeting. I stood. "I should get back to work."

Georgianne turned to me. "Thank you for keeping Quinton company for me. I know I can always count on you."

"Yes," he said. "I would like to continue our discussion later."

Was he being polite, or did he really want to see me again? The mere thought had my cheeks flushing. "That would be nice."

I turned to Georgianne. "It sounds like Margaret, Layton, and the others at the foundation are going to be very busy today. Should I send food?"

Georgianne gave me a warm smile. "I already thought about that. Layton said he didn't think it would be necessary. There is only so much they can do at the moment. I want to talk to Layton first, but I think we may see what we can do to send food to the victims."

"Just let me know what needs to be done."

"I will."

Quinton pulled his phone out of his breast pocket again. "If you'll excuse me, I'm going to call Father and see if he has any more insight on the matter."

I watched the prince cross the restaurant with strong, confident strides. He sat at a stool at the counter and dialed the phone.

When he spoke, he did so in his native language. Even though I didn't understand a word he said, I could hear the emotion. It appeared to me he was talking to someone about something more personal and painful than a country miles away from his own.

Either Quinton was more affected by the tragedy than he immediately let on, or Georgianne's hunch was right and there was more to his visit than he'd originally indicated.

CHAPTER TWO

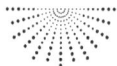

J hadn't had much time to think about Quinton since Layton arrived and the three of them left for their house. Customers had shuffled in and out of the bistro all morning and afternoon. Stepping in to fill Georgianne's shoes—as well as managing my own job—had kept me busy.

As we approached mid-afternoon, we were hitting a lull. I felt like I could catch my breath, except the memories of Quinton's flirty smile and broad chest distracted me again. I tried to shake away the lust-filled daydreams. What was the point? In a day or two the prince would jet back to Ronaria, and I'd probably never see him again.

I picked up the clipboard from Georgianne's desk and headed to the cooler and stock room to take inventory. With the expansion in business over the last year, we'd gone to a weekly ordering system for supplies. I knew Georgianne planned to place an order today but would be distracted with their house guest. I wanted to do whatever I could to make the business run smoothly.

I was halfway through the task when I heard her voice in

the kitchen. Not even a moment later she found me in the stock room.

One look at her face and I knew—as she'd expected—Quinton had delivered bad news. I set the clipboard down on a stack of boxes and went to her. "What is it?"

She looked pale as she gripped the edge of the shelving, wrapping her fingers tightly around the metal. "Layton and I are headed to Ronaria first thing in the morning."

So soon? "Why so quickly? What about your work and your father?"

Georgianne's mouth gaped, and she waved a hand in front of her face. "Oh! No! It wasn't what I thought." She paused and swallowed hard. Her eyes suddenly glossy with tears. "It's much worse."

The news Quinton delivered—whatever it was—had obviously shattered her. I slipped my arm around Georgianne's shoulder and led her back through the kitchen to her office. Once there, I closed the door.

Georgianne collapsed in the chair behind her desk and reached for a tissue, dabbing it at her eyes.

"What is it? Is there some way I can help?"

She swallowed hard, and looked up at me. "Do you remember Delilah?"

When Layton had come to the queen's child welfare summit a year and a half ago, he'd brought several orphans from his country. One—an orphaned teenager—served as a chaperone to the other children and an assistant to Layton. "I do."

"She's been diagnosed with a brain tumor. Quinton says that so far none of the doctors she's seen are willing to operate. The size and position severely limit the treatment options."

I felt as the world was slipping away and reached for the edge of the desk. When Delilah had been here in the bistro,

I'd seen a reflection of myself in her. She'd been fiercely protective of Layton—the one person in the world she felt she could rely on—and it'd taken Georgianne time and patience to win the girl's trust and eventual approval.

After Layton's six-month sabbatical from his position in Ronaria, he'd decided to take a position in Queen Margaret's charitable foundation, making what I thought was a permanent move to Montgomery. However, as I'd learned from Quinton, Layton's entire family considered his move a temporary arrangement.

I leaned back against the wall. My stomach hurt as if someone had punched me, knocking the wind out of me. "There are no words."

"Layton is a wreck. He feels so guilty for not being with her through the diagnosis. Quinton has found a specialist in the type of cancer she has. The doctor is being flown in tomorrow. We are leaving first thing in the morning so Layton can be there when Delilah is examined." She turned to the desk and tried to regain some composure. "I'm leaving you in complete control. I don't know how long I will be gone. I think we can trust Myra to run the shifts you do not work. Don't you agree?"

I stepped behind Georgianne and laid my hands on her shoulders. "You shouldn't be here. I know what to do. Go to Layton."

She reached up and gripped my hand. "I know you will handle everything just fine." She covered her face with her hands and began sobbing again. "He must hate me right now."

"Who? Layton? You know that's not true."

She turned the chair and looked up at me. "I knew what his work and those children meant to him, but I let him give the job to his aunt and come here for me. Over what? This business?"

A wave of nausea rolled through me. I'd been preoccupied with what it would do to me when they went to Ronaria, I hadn't really thought about what Layton had given up. "You work is important to you, and he still helps children."

"He considers the ones in Ronaria to be *his*. He loves and cares for each one. I don't know how he could ever forgive me for causing him to miss out on the last year and half of Delilah's short life."

I bent over and hugged Georgianne's neck. My heart shredded thinking about the girl Layton always described as a handful. "Neither one of you had any way of knowing this would happen. You can't second guess your choices."

Georgianne patted her back. "I know you're right. There is no looking back, no changing the past." She found her feet and wiped the tears from her cheeks with the back of her hand. "We are leaving for Ronaria before dawn breaks, so I'll need you to do tomorrow's baking. I'll leave it up to you who you want to have come in and assist."

I picked up a pad of paper from her desk and a pen. "Do you want to give me a schedule? What should I bake on which days?"

She forced a smile. "You bake with me every day. Use your best judgement. If you get in a jam, you can reach me by phone. Quinton has kindly offered to stay here and help Margaret manage the earthquake support to Italy. He said he would check in with you often. I told him it was unnecessary, but he insisted. Humor him, please. He wants to feel useful."

Just the mention of Quinton's name had my heart rate quickening. It made me proud to know Georgianne trusted me to handle things, but a piece of me longed to see him. "I'm sure both you and Layton feel better knowing Quinton will be here to rely on."

She took my hands and gave them a squeeze. "I'm grateful Layton's family thinks enough of me and respects what I do enough to offer, but Quinton is not a restaurateur. Besides, I know there isn't a thing that could come up that you wouldn't know how to handle. As far as Layton's work, I'm sure Quinton will be able to help coordinate relief efforts, and it does ease Layton's guilt of leaving during a crisis."

"We'll manage. You just focus on Delilah."

"We will. Now, do you think we have an extra loaf of bread I can take home to have with dinner tonight."

"Of course. How about some dessert?"

"I'll take a few lemon tarts. Maybe Quinton will like those."

"It's so odd. He *really* doesn't like sweets?"

She shrugged. "I know. Crazy, right?" After a pause, she continued. "I sometimes wonder if it's more about not wanting to eat unhealthily than not liking the food. I think it goes back to his days in the ballet."

It made a lot of sense, and made me wonder if his cool detached behavior when he first arrived didn't have more to do with missing the ballet and resenting his life now "That could be. Does he dance at all?"

Georgianne gave a nod. "Layton says he uses it as a form of exercise but honors their father's request and doesn't perform anymore. I know he travels to Slovakia a lot. He insists they are business trips, but he has so many friends there, I'm sure he misses them when he's away. I feel bad for him really."

"Everyone should have the opportunity to follow their dreams."

"Layton, Quinton, and the rest of their family take their positions seriously." She paused and brushed away a stray tear from her cheek. "It amazes me every day the way Layton has sacrificed for us. I'm ashamed I've taken advantage of his kindness. Now, look what it might have cost him."

I set the box of lemon tarts on the counter and wrapped

18

an arm around Georgianne's neck. "He loves you. Hold on to hope. Maybe this new doctor will be able to help Delilah."

"I pray so."

To lift the mood, I tried to shift the conversation. "Did Quinton give you the housewarming present yet?"

"Did he tell you about the paintings? They are so beautiful. They were hanging them when I left."

"He showed me pictures. They are striking."

"The artist is just beginning his career. He's so lucky to have gained Quinton's notice. It will bring good things to him."

CHAPTER THREE

$\mathcal{I}$ pushed the tray of apple blossoms into the oven and wiped my hands on my apron. A quick glance at the clock told me Georgianne and Layton were on their way to Ronaria. Just the thought of their trip caused tears to spring to my eyes.

Yes, I was worried being back home with his family and his dear Delilah's illness might cause Layton to question his choices. He might push Georgianne to make the inevitable move, but it was more than that.

My heart broke for Delilah.

When I'd heard she was gravely ill, I could only imagine myself in the same position—scared and alone with no family to turn to.

I'd been in her shoes. I knew she wore a tough exterior because the world could be a hard, lonely place to an orphan who had long outgrown the infant or toddler years.

I knew if I really needed them, Georgianne and James would stand by my side, just as she and Layton were going to Delilah now. Still, it emphasized how lonely my life *really* was and escalated my desire to find a life partner with whom I could raise a family of my own.

When would my Prince Charming come to me like Georgianne's had?

My mind wandered to Quinton, and the flutter of butterfly wings returned to my stomach. What was it about the man that made my head light? Besides the obvious: his magnificent good looks. Or maybe the fantasy persona I'd attached to the man I'd watched in all those internet videos. Still, something about the short time we'd spent together—especially with the man who'd relaxed, smiled, and shown me photos of paintings on his phone—had me yearning for more. I hoped Quinton would be stopping by like Georgianne suggested he might.

After checking the ovens, I crossed to the main dining room. I moved from one machine to the other, turning them on and making sure they were ready to begin brewing. I pressed buttons to start the main pots—already prepped with light, medium, and dark roast coffees.

A light knock turned my attention to the door. Quinton stood just outside, dressed much more casual than the day before. He wore a pair of sage green pants and a beige polo shirt. Dark glasses shielded his eyes from the early morning sun. When he saw he had my attention, he smiled.

My palms begin to sweat as if I were back in the kitchen pulling trays from the oven.

I crossed the room and unlocked the door, holding it for him. "Good morning, Prince—" I stopped midsentence, remembering how he'd insisted I not use his title while addressing him.

Still, he removed his glasses and leveled his gaze on me. "Please."

His intense gaze captivated me. I looked away, feeling my cheeks warm with embarrassment. "Quinton. I'll try to

21

remember. Georgianne said you might stop by. Did they get off all right?"

"Yes. I took them to the airport this morning and stayed until the plane was off the ground. Georgianne mentioned you'd have a delivery for the castle this morning. Since I am headed there anyway, I thought I deliver it."

"Thank you. I was going to send Marcus as soon as he arrived, but that would leave me shorthanded. The order is still in the oven. Can I get you something to eat while you wait?"

"Georgianne fixed so much food this morning, I swear I won't have to eat for days. An espresso would be lovely, though." He paused, dipping his head to meet my stare. "But please. I can get it myself."

I turned—afraid I would melt under the intensity of his stare. "I'll get it. These machines can be complicated."

Get yourself together. I steeled myself as I walked past him, pausing in front of the brewer. I stared blankly at the settings and buttons for a moment, before reaching for the correct container and taking it to the coffee grinder.

I could feel Quinton tighten the distance between us, standing at my back while I filled the small metal box. "I'm supposed to be helping you, not creating more work. I fear Georgianne would be angry for being a distraction. Show me how to run the equipment, so I can do it next time."

A lump formed in my throat as I tried to push away a fantasy that entailed him wrapping his arms around my waist and pressing those thin pink lips to the side of my neck, or lifting me, like I had watched him do with tiny little ballerinas. I could almost feel his hands pressed firmly against my ribcage, and struggled to regain my focus on the machine in front of me. "The grinder has several settings. For espresso, you want a course grind."

Once done I turned, but Quinton held his ground and I

found myself eye-to-muscular chest. "Did you use a bold blend?"

I found myself staring at his mouth, craving its caress. Though his words seemed innocuous, his reflection had me quivering. "I did."

He stepped to one side, his gaze still much too intense for a training session. "Good. I like vibrant flavor."

He's talking about coffee. I reminded myself as I twisted back to the machine, walking him through the remaining steps. I pushed the start button. "That's it, in a few moments, your espresso will be ready."

"Seems easy enough."

"It is. Help yourself when it's done brewing. I'll get the castle's order out of the oven and packaged up."

I walked through the door, grateful for the solace of the kitchen and a bit of space from Quinton. When he stood close to me I felt like a teenager again, struggling to breath because the air was hot with electrical sparks.

I didn't want my attraction to be a downfall, causing me to do something stupid—like I had when I'd fallen head-over-heels in my high school days. The object of my desires then had convinced me it was okay to steal a car and take it to a concert one town over. Not that I thought Quinton had crime on his mind, but making a fool of myself in front of Georgianne's soon-to-be in-laws would disappoint her. She was counting on me, and I wouldn't let her down.

I pulled the trays from the oven, depositing them in the rack. I then wheeled the large frame to the prep table where I'd already prepared the boxes and lined them with waxed paper.

I heard the door swing open and looked up to see Quinton. Once in the kitchen, he leaned against the wall.

"Only employees are allowed in here. I don't know if Georgianne would like this."

He laughed as he approached the table, with the same confident swagger he'd used while on the phone the day before. One that said he owned any room he entered. "I am here to help—both you and my brother's fiancée."

I kept my eyes on my work. Something about the way he acted—as though he'd be comfortable ruling a nation—amped up the heat between us. The sweet and vulnerable side—the man who supported his brother and shared pictures of his art—was just as appealing.

Really, did a girl stand a chance?

"This isn't the first time I've been left in charge. To the best of my knowledge, Georgianne hasn't been disappointed yet."

He set his cup on the prep table and reached out, brushing my forearm. "Did I indicate she was? I didn't mean to."

No. my frustration comes from this unexplainable attraction. I shook my head. "You didn't say anything like that, but you are here this morning. I assume to make sure everything is handled to Georgianne's standards."

"It's not that. I swear. She trusts you."

"Is it that you don't?" Why was I protesting his presence? I *was* glad he was there. Maybe too glad. It was affecting my ability to think straight.

"I just want to help. My brother is hurting, worried sick about his charge, and there isn't a single thing I can do at this point to assist with Delilah's health. I thought if I could make things easier on you, it would leave Georgianne to support him."

Guilt flooded my gut. I needed to quit jumping at shadows and get my head on straight. Quinton was here for a few days, and then he would be gone. There was no point in falling head-over-heels. But what about Layton? Was he going to whisk Georgianne away at this point. "Does Layton plan to return to Ronaria? For good I mean."

"I have not discussed it with him, but I assume he will once he and Georgianne marry."

"Why do you think that?"

"Ronaria is his home, and our people expect him to be there. To serve. Whether he accepts it or not, Father will ensure we all live up to our obligations."

"This is Georgianne's home. Her father lives here, and her business is well established."

"Layton's bride becomes my sister. Her father becomes family, too. Their home will be our home. I know the bistro is important to her, but once they are married, she will be expected to follow suit and take a role in service to Ronaria."

"What if she doesn't want to?"

"Feelings are of no consequence. I'm sorry it is that way, but Layton is aware of Father's will. He should have explained all of this to Georgianne before now."

Quinton gave no indication he was talking about himself, but given what Georgianne had told me, his feelings on the subject must run deep. "Maybe it's not my place to say anything, but I think people should have the right to pursue their own lives. Follow their hearts and live accordingly."

Quinton took a deep breath and rested his chin on his fist. After a moment of what appeared to be deep contemplation, a smile lightened his face, and a chuckle escaped his lips. "I like talking to you, Isabel. You are not only intelligent, but compassionate." He picked up his cup and sipped from his espresso. "I'm sure Montgomery has been a lovely change of pace for my brother. It is his temperament to sit behind a desk and work directly with children for their benefit— without the watchful and adoring eye of his public. But he also knows we are born into our responsibilities. We cannot be selfish. We must repay the debt we owe our people with service."

"Was it really that easy for you to give up your dreams?"

He stepped closer to me. "What dreams do you think I gave up?"

"Dancing. I've watched videos of you with the Slovakian ballet, before your father made you give it up. Excuse me, but he sounds a bit tyrannical to me."

His posture softened, and he tipped his head. "I can see how it would appear, but my siblings and I have been taught from a young age about how blessed we are to be royal. I knew what would be expected of me and when I would have to take up my service."

"But what about dancing? Don't you miss it?"

He paused. "I love to dance. In fact, I still do."

"Georgianne said you don't perform at all anymore."

"It does not matter who is watching. Dancing is an art, same as painting or drawing. It is an expression of emotion through movements of the body. When I'm alone, I do it for exercise. When I'm in Slovakia, the company allows me to rehearse with them."

"You are an incredible dancer, and your father never should have made you stop." I placed the lids on the boxes and stacked them. "These are ready."

He closed the remaining distance and touched my arm again. The small amount of air between us became thick. "I appreciate your thoughts, but it much more complicated than what it seems. May I explain it to you over lunch?"

"I will be working, and we are too busy over the lunch hour for me to sit and talk. But you are welcome to come here and eat. In fact, I know Georgianne would insist on it."

"What about you, Isabel? Would you like it too?"

I felt my cheeks flush and gave the large cart a tug,

intending to fill the display cases before opening the bistro for the day. "You are welcome to eat here."

"That does not answer my question. Would you *like* me too?"

I swallowed hard. The thoughts of him leaning in just a little closer and kissing me flooded me. I couldn't form words, so I merely nodded.

He grazed my cheek with his knuckles. "Good, because I would like to spend more time with you too. Do you have an invoice for the delivery?"

I picked up the paper off the prep table and offered it to him. "Tell Garan I will send someone over after lunch to pick up a check."

He folded the invoice into quarters and slid it into his pocket. "That will not be necessary."

"Georgianne and the queen have an agreement. They pay their invoices upon receipt."

He smirked. "What I meant to say is I will bring the payment when I return for lunch."

CHAPTER FOUR

I smiled at the bus boy and held the kitchen door as he maneuvered the large tray through. I then continued on my way to the cash register, inserted the key, turned it, and punched the numbers to start running sales reports.

I believed Georgianne would be calling—sooner rather than later—and I wanted hard sales numbers so she could dictate the baking for the next day.

I found my gaze straying toward the door, hoping Quinton would come back for lunch as he promised. It took every ounce of concentration to shake off my desire for the man who had a way of tantalizing me and focus on the tape being spit out of the machine.

Don't forget he believes Layton should return to Ronaria and Georgianne should close this shop.

If all of that happens, how will you be able to care for a child?

I chastised myself for the thoughts. I was being selfish and blaming Quinton for a system he'd fallen victim to as well.

Just because he'd allowed his father to push him to give up the ballet didn't mean it was right for the situation to repeat itself with Layton. I reminded myself Layton and Georgianne had flown to Ronaria for Delilah, and chances were his father wouldn't use this time to discuss his future. But it would come up eventually, and I needed to have a discussion with James about my adoption plans.

Jana stood at the end of the counter, wiping down the menus with a damp cloth. "Have you heard from Georgianne today?"

"No, but I imagine Layton wanted to get to Delilah as soon as they landed."

The woman sighed and shook her head. "It's so sad."

I nodded as I ran a finger down the strip of paper trying to analyze the batches of numbers. Georgianne diligently used her business degree to scrutinize sales trends and patterns, but I'd found it near impossible to predict with any kind of certainty how much of a particular item would sell. One days it seemed like everyone in town craved chocolate, and the next it might be the lemon tarts that flew off the shelves.

"We've been busy today," Jana commented.

I couldn't disagree. "The case is looking pretty bare, we won't have much waste. Did the castle call in an order for tomorrow?"

"Not yet. Do you expect one?"

"Not exactly. Prince Quinton delivered one this morning. He said he would bring payment back with him when he came for lunch. I didn't see him. I know the foundation is busy trying to coordinate help for the earthquake victims. They must have worked through lunch."

Jana shook her head and clicked her tongue. "So horrible. Did you see the images of the orphanage on the news last night?"

I could only nod my head. "I want to help but feel so helpless."

"I wouldn't worry about the invoice. You know the queen will pay."

I opened the register and began counting it down, placing the funds from the day's sales into a deposit bag. "I'm not worried about that. I just want to make sure everything is done the way Georgianne would want it."

Jana brought the stack of breakfast and lunch menus behind the counter and placed them in the proper place beneath it. "Do you want me to set up the dining room for dinner?"

I checked my watch. "It's a bit early. I expect a few late lunch stragglers." Closing the register, I tucked the deposit bag beneath my arm. "Why don't you clean the display cases. The pies should be cooled enough to place in there once you're done."

"Will do." Janna pointed toward the door. "There's the prince now."

I couldn't stop my gaze from following her point. Sure enough, he was walking up the street with his confident power stride. My heart began to beat wildly. "Start a double shot of espresso for him, please. I will put this in the safe and be right back to take his order."

I quickly moved through the kitchen, checking on the desserts and pastries that were being brought out of the ovens. After locking the cash into the safe, I retraced my steps, pausing briefly to go over the specials for the evening with Marcus. I could concentrate on nothing but getting back to Quinton, though.

When I walked back into the dining room, he looked up over his espresso cup from his place at the counter, meeting my stare with his brooding one. He set the cup down and gave me a wide smile.

As I approached, he slipped an envelope across the counter. "I have something for you, Miss Isabel."

I peeked in to confirm the total was right and then stepped to my left and punched the buttons to open the register. "Thank you."

"You will be pleased to know I spoke with Layton shortly after their plane landed. Their flight was routine, and they were headed straight to the hospital. Georgianne wanted me to inform you it would most likely be late tonight before she has time to call."

"Thanks for letting me know." I crossed back to stand in front of him. "It's late. Did you already eat?"

He shook his head. "We've been so focused on coordinating relief efforts to Italy, time got away from all of us." He slid a finger down the menu Jana must have given him. "Am I too late to get this kale and Brussels sprout salad and a cup of chowder please."

"Not at all." I walked back to the point of sale machine and tapped in his order. "I saw the images on the news. I can't imagine the orphanage being salvaged."

"The building has been condemned. All the children are displaced. My father has joined with your queen and king to help with the relief. Our plane is now being loaded with supplies and will go to Lecce later tonight. Tomorrow, twenty children will be flown here. Half will go on to Ronaria."

"You were able to make room in Montgomery's and Ronaria's orphanages?"

"Space is an issue, but what choice do we have? These children need a place to lay their heads. The details have kept me very busy. I fear I'm not as competent at this as Layton."

"Don't sell yourself short. You've accomplished so much in a short time."

"I know enough about how businesses and governments are run to tug at the needed strings," he conceded. "Do you see. This is why it's important for my siblings and me to do the things we do. Had I not made dancing a hobby and learned these skills, I would have been of no use today."

I busied myself by getting him a set of silverware and pouring a glass of water as I spoke. "I never meant to imply the work you and Layton do is not necessary or wonderful. My question is, does it fill your heart?"

"The work I do on my arts council is very rewarding. It may not be as life changing as what Layton does here—"

"Music and dance and painting—all the arts—are very important. Music was one of my only escapes when I was in the orphanage, and when Viviana decided I was to take some dance classes, it was the beginning of what finally turned me around."

Quinton's mouth dropped. "I wasn't aware—"

"I don't like to talk about it."

He took another sip of his coffee. "You said Viviana decided. You ended up living with them?"

"Off and on in my late teens." I hated talking about those years and was surprised how easily it'd been to admit it to him. "I was nearly ten when my mother lost her custodial rights to me. I was in and out of foster homes over the years, mostly because I'd become rebellious and more than a handful for those who would take me in. That was, until James and Viviana.

"I understand so much more now. You and Georgianne were raised as sisters, and you are worried about her moving to Ronaria. You will miss her. She is a lovely woman and— I'm guessing—a dear friend."

"She is *my* family. The only one I know. When I turned eighteen, I needed a job, and Georgianne gave me one. As her business has done better, she's promoted me and given me raises. She may not *be* my sister, but she *is*. Do you know what I mean?"

He leaned across the counter, closing the distance

between us and lowering his voice. "Completely. I had no idea before now."

"If Georgianne goes to Ronaria, I believe it will be only be a matter of time before James follows. I will once again be left alone."

Quinton leaned back in the chair and took a deep breath. "I now understand why this upsets you so. But if what you say is true, then they must care for you in the same way you do them. Time and miles are hard, but nothing comes between family. They will simply be a few hours away by plane."

The same warmth he showed when discussing Delilah or the earthquake victims he now showed me. Mingled with the warmth was a look I knew all too well. A look I detested: pity.

Which was why I needed to keep the *real* reason I couldn't lose this job to myself. If I were going to adopt, I needed to know I could take care of a child on my own. It was a good thing I hadn't yet mentioned my intentions to anyone but James. Until I knew for sure Georgianne would not be closing the bistro, I'd have to put my plans on hold.

I needed to clarify I was strong and self-sufficient. I wanted him to stop looking at me like I was someone who needed saving.

"I can take care of myself, you know."

I instantly regretted my harsh tone. Quinton hadn't said a thing to deserve my defensiveness.

"I'm certain you can." He shifted his weight in the chair, his focus laser-sharp on me. I could almost see the wheels of his mind spinning.

Jana appeared from the kitchen with his lunch and placed the dishes in front of him.

He politely thanked her before taking a spoonful of soup.

After swallowing, he gave his attention back to me. "I would like to take you out to dinner tonight."

Why? Because he thought I needed to be cared for? "I don't know if that's a good idea."

"Why not?"

"You're my boss's soon-to-be brother-in-law. Somehow, it feels like it would cross some line."

The corner of his mouth hiked up. "I am here helping my brother and his fiancée in a country where you and the queen are the only people I know. I'm not crazy about eating alone and would love some company."

How silly of me to think he was asking for a date. I was not Georgianne. There was no fairytale ending for me. No matter how much I longed for more from Quinton, it was companionship he wanted. "I get off in an hour, but I have a few errands to run."

"With this late lunch, I would be fine with a late dinner."

"Should I meet you back here?"

He shook his head. "No. The food is tempting, but I want to get to know you outside of your work."

You do? Was it possible this was some sort of date? "Where would you like to meet?"

"Where can I pick you up?"

How much could I trust Quinton? Or these feelings that were making my head light? He was a Prince. And Layton's brother. I knew would be safe with him, even if my heart was in danger.

I bit my lip, dug deep, and told him my address.

CHAPTER FIVE

*B*efore Quinton had finished his lunch, my replacement for the evening shift arrived. I gathered my things—including the deposit for the bank—and, after leaving very specific orders for the staff, said my goodbyes.

I went about my usual chores, trying not to think too hard about the planned dinner with the prince. Of course, I wanted to believe his invitation was about more than not wanting to eat alone, but the prospect he was just as interested in me as I was in him was more than a little scary.

If it had seemed inconceivable Georgianne would be swept away by a prince, it felt impossible for me. So, until I had a reason to believe differently, I would work under the assumption tonight was about entertaining Layton's family in his and Georgianne's absence.

Even though I should go home and start getting ready—he'd told me he was taking me to one of the nicest restaurants in town—I couldn't help myself and made a stop at very familiar stomping grounds, walking up the large stone steps to the orphanage.

Once inside, I twisted to the right and entered James's office. His secretary, Miss Tillie, greeted me with a warm smile. "We weren't expecting you today, Isabel, but it's always a pleasure."

It was kind of her to say those words, even though we both knew they hadn't always been true. In my formative and rebellious years, I often saw a much sterner side to her and the other employees here.

It took time, but with James patient, persistent interest in me, I'd softened. Time and life experience had taught me to appreciate the people who'd been there for me—even when I had no desire to be here.

In the last year, it'd become a mission of mine to pay it forward. I volunteered a few days a week. I helped children with their studies, assisted the kitchen staff in meal preparation, and even helped housekeeping with the laundry. Wherever they were shorthanded, I'd jump in to help the agency, but most of all my goal was to help the children.

"I hadn't planned to volunteer, but I hoped James might have a few free moments."

She looked at the phone. "His line is not lit up. He's been occupied with planning for the Italian children's arrival tomorrow, but I will let him know you are here. I know if it's all possible, he'd like to visit."

I nodded my appreciation and twisted my hands as she slipped into James's office. I'd had numerous conversations over the last month about adopting. Though they'd grown more serious in recent weeks, we hadn't actually taken steps forward.

Until Quinton waltzed into the bistro and flipped my life upside down, I'd been sure I wanted to give a child a home, I just hadn't picked a specific one to start the paperwork on.

Now I just wasn't sure about my own financial security. Adopting was supposed to be about providing love and security. I couldn't offer that to myself, let alone a child, without my job.

Miss Tillie reappeared with James at her side.

"Isabel! Come in!" He opened his arms.

I stepped into his warm embrace. "You're not too busy?"

"For you, never. Can you bring us some coffee, Winifred?"

I turned to Miss Tillie. "None for me. I won't be here long."

I took the chair in front of his desk.

"Did you come by to visit the children?"

I bit my lips and reluctantly shook my head. I thought this discussion would be easy to have. Now that I sat in front of James, finding the right words proved harder than I thought. "I fear I must put on hold my decision about adopting a child."

He dipped his chin and took a moment before speaking. "I know this is a big decision, which is why I advised you to take your time making it, but I thought you'd worked through your concerns and were now certain."

"Don't get me wrong, I'm committed to becoming a foster parent and adopting. I'm just not sure the timing is right."

The corner of his mouth twitched, like it always did when he was amused. Still I could see he fought to remain stoic. "I see. What is it about *this moment* that has you concerned?"

"Georgianne's trip to Ronaria." It was the most direct answer, even though it didn't scratch the surface of my turbulent emotions.

"I would think she'd be home in a couple weeks at the most. It's a short-term delay then? If so, I'd suggest moving forward with the paperwork. Even if everything falls right into place, it will still be a month, maybe two, before all the ducks are in a row."

Maybe I could keep my deepest fears under a veil with Quinton, but I couldn't do that with James. "You don't understand. Her trip has me concerned because I'm unsure of my future after she and Layton marry. Quinton seems to think they will relocate to Ronaria."

"I'm not sure what their timeline is, but Layton cannot stay away forever."

"What will happen to *Viviana's Bistro*—my job? How can I afford to care for a child without an income?"

The absolute terror must have shown on my face, because James stood, rounded the desk and squatted before me, taking my hands. "Take a deep breath, Isabel."

I did what he said.

"Okay. Another one."

I couldn't stop the giggle as I inhaled the air deep in my lungs and slowly let it go. He knew me, understood my fears, and had a way of calming me down as no one else ever had.

"You are a very valued employee to Georgianne. She couldn't successfully run the bistro without you."

"It's not true."

"It is. She's said it more than once. Life with Layton is already different than what her life looked like eighteen months ago. It will continue to grow and change when they get married."

"I know."

"But Georgianne isn't changing. Do you think she would do something so sudden without warning you? She knows your very livelihood depends on the bistro."

I hadn't thought about it from that point of view, but James was right. Georgianne talked about everything with me, she wouldn't keep secrets about the fate of the restaurant. "No. She wouldn't."

"I can't promise Viviana's, as we know it, will always be there, but I can assure you Georgianne will keep you completely informed with what's going on. No changes will happen abruptly."

The words sounded sweet coming from him. I know he said them to calm me, but also knew the issues didn't have black-and-white borders. The lines were fuzzy and blurred. "In a perfect world, things would happen like you say. But look at poor Delilah, do you think she planned to get a brain tumor? What about the poor children in Italy? Do you think they knew an earthquake would destroy the closest thing to a home they have?"

"Are you worried something bad will happen to you?"

"You can't promise me it won't. I thought I was ready to adopt on my own. I thought I was strong enough to do this without a husband, but am I being selfish? If I lose my job or get sick, who would my child be able to depend on?"

"You!"

"And I would fail her or him."

"No! No, you wouldn't. It's awful, but the hard times you're talking about happen to parents all the time. People get sick, lose jobs, and get in accidents. They are still parents. They still take care of their children."

"They usually have a partner to help them."

"In some cases, yes, but you know not all. The things you are worried about are valid, and I do think you need to take some time to consider them, but don't let fear be your response. You are a strong woman. Smart too. And you have an amazing capacity and desire to give a home to children who need it. If life decides to take a twisted turn, you will figure out how to maneuver through it. Married or not—and I believe someone will come along and see how wonderful you are—you have a support system of people who love you and will always be there for you."

I squeezed his hand. "Thank you, James. I know you are right. Forget I came in here. I know I want to move forward."

"In that case"—James righted himself and reached to his desk, shuffling through the papers—"I'd planned on bringing these to you tomorrow. I need you to fill out some additional paperwork."

I took the folder and flipped it open. "What is this?"

"Background information for the home study."

I skimmed through the pages, taken aback by how personal some of the questions were. "Will you come out and do that?"

"No. A social worker will do the visit."

With James, I felt I had an advocate on my side. A social worker might examine my past with more scrutiny and not understand my desire to do this now, while I was still a single woman. They would probably have all the same concerns that had been haunting me since learning of Delilah's illness. "You know I can take care of a child."

He gave a curt nod. "I just said that. But I'm not going to lie to you. There are some issues that could stand in the way."

"I'm a single woman."

He nodded. "The laws prohibiting singles from adopting were modified a few years ago, but that doesn't mean opinions of those in the system have kept up."

"You said they can't deny me because I'm not married."

"It can't be the reason listed for the denial. We know you're climbing a tough road here, but we have a plan."

"Dot every *i* and cross every *t*?"

"Leave nothing else to chance. Don't give them any other reason. I, of course, will write a recommendation for you. I'm sure Georgianne and Layton will too."

"I don't want to impose on them."

"As your boss, you will need Georgianne to write a referral. Your work ethic and the responsibilities she entrusts you with are all pluses. A personal recommendation from the Prince of Ronaria—who is so well known for his work in children's welfare—is something that will be hard to ignore."

"But, it seems too much to ask."

"You know Georgianne and Layton won't hesitate. I'm surprised they haven't offered to do it all ready."

"They don't know about my intentions to adopt yet. You're the only one I've told."

His lips flattened to a thin line, and his forehead wrinkled. "You're going to have to talk to Georgianne. It's going to be imperative to show your employer is aware of you becoming a parent and will allow you flexibility in your schedule when necessary."

I hated putting such an important outcome into another person's hands. If I'd learned nothing else over the years, it was that trusting other people resulted in getting hurt. The only person I could count on was me. I'd taken care of myself —for the most part—from the time I was taken away from my mother. Except for the stretches of time I'd been placed in James's home.

As soon as I'd grown comfortable—believed this time they might ask me to stay—I'd be placed in yet another foster home. Sure enough, in time, I'd find a way to disappoint my new foster parents—proving there was absolutely no one who could love me for who I was—and I'd be sent back.

I knew what it was like to be an older child in a battered and broken system. I could be understanding of what the kids were going through.

James was right. I possessed the strength to do this, and I wouldn't fail. Someone's future depended on me sticking to my guns.

CHAPTER SIX

When the waiter appeared at the table, Quinton ordered a bottle of wine and an appetizer from the menu. When we were alone again, he leveled his gaze across the table.

I withered under his stare. Turbulent emotions lived there. Every arch of his back or lift of his leg were gestures I'd watched countless times online. When I'd felt angry, lost, and disillusioned with the world, I'd call up one of his videos on my computer or phone. Watching him exorcise angst through his movements lifted the negativity from me.

Knowing he'd given it up, made me sad. I looked down, flattening the napkin on my lap. "I'm sorry. I haven't been much company this evening. I should have followed my gut instinct and cancelled."

"For what it's worth, I'm glad you didn't."

"Even if I'm being moody?"

"I don't think you've been glum, just a little quiet." He leaned forward and spoke in a low, flirty tone. "Have I told you how beautiful you look tonight?"

"You have. More than once." I fidgeted with my bracelet

and tapped my foot. With each flirtatious advance Quinton made, I feared I would do something to chase him away.

He straightened in the chair. "I get the feeling you don't hear that very often."

I shrugged. "My focus for the last couple of years has been getting my life in order. I've dated here and there, but I haven't been looking for a serious relationship."

He gave a slight nod, giving me the impression he understood how I felt.

The waiter reappeared with the bottle of wine. He opened it and poured a small amount in Quinton's glass. The prince went through the motions of examining, sniffing, and tasting the wine, before nodding his approval.

Only then did the waiter pour some into each of our glasses before leaving the table.

Alone again, the focus came back on me, but words seemed to escape him.

I couldn't take the silence any longer. "What about you? Are you in a relationship?"

"No. Not now. Not for some time."

"I can't imagine someone as good-looking and kind as you lacks for offers."

He chuckled. "I guess I'm supposed to be flattered by the compliments."

"You're not?"

He leaned back in the chair and fiddled with the button of his suit jacket. "The offers, as you say, are plentiful, but it can be difficult. There are many demands on my life. My personal time can be very limited. That is difficult for some to understand."

"Was it easier when you were with the ballet?"

The waiter returned with their appetizer—a plate of asparagus that had been roasted in a balsamic reduction. We placed our dinner orders, and the server disappeared again.

He rubbed his chin for a few seconds. He seemed to be reaching—searching—for the right words. "When I danced, my time was just as limited. I devoted as many hours a day to my rehearsing as I do with my duties today. I was three years old when my mother thought dancing might be a good way to *expend my bountiful energy*. From the first class, I was hooked, and even those early instructors believed I had promise. By the time I was seven, I was rehearsing seven, eight, sometimes nine hours a day."

I'd been so preoccupied with how Ronaria's king had ripped dancing from his son, I hadn't thought about what Quinton had sacrificed to dance in the first place. "You didn't have a childhood."

He slid his hand across the table until his fingertips brushed mine. "I never thought of it that way. Dancing was hard work, but it brought me such joy. Being royal is a solitary life anyway. Our parents had to scrutinize everyone we tried to become friends with, but they didn't have to do that with the music."

"I can tell you miss it very much."

"I do." His lips puckered, and he shifted his weight in the chair. "Why does it make you so sad?"

"You gave your life to something that made you so happy, and your father took it away from you like it was nothing."

He bowed his head, shaking it. "No. You don't understand. I miss dancing, but I have no regrets. My parents raised us to know what was expected. My brothers and I choose the way we serve our country, but we've always known we will serve. Not for one moment did I think I would be allowed to dance forever."

"Still, it must have been hard."

He nodded. "Of course it was, but I still dance. I am grateful for this. What is not so easy is knowing when a person is genuine—when they like me. Sometimes a woman may seem interested in getting acquainted, but in her heart, she longs to be close to the dancer or the prince—not me."

I could empathize. I often found myself questioning a person's intentions, but it had to be a hundred times worse for him. I merely feared getting hurt. He had to worry about being used for his wealth and position. He also had to consider his family. "You must get lonely."

He gave a curt nod. "Sometimes. When I'm really busy it's hard to notice."

I felt another connection drawn between us. I used my work at the bistro to distract myself too. "Work is a wonderful thing."

"What is it about dating that scares you?"

Scared? "I'm not afraid!"

Too defensive?

Yeah! Take it down a notch. I warned myself.

"You're not?" His eyes danced, and his tone was nearly musical.

At least he was entertained by my barricades. I tried to keep my walls in place, but they crumbled around him. "I think it has to do with how I was shuffled around through my teens. One foster home after the other, none of them permanent. I now know I created most of the issues myself, but I think the idea that no one could really care about the real me got deeper ingrained with each rejection."

He slid his hand across the table, laying his hand palm out in front of me. I hesitated at first but then gave him what I felt he wanted. He wrapped his fingers tight around mine.

My hand tingled in his.

He stroked the side of my hand with his thumb softly. "Have you showed me the real you?"

"I don't hide who I am anymore. Georgianne and James have helped me overcome that. Viviana did too. God rest her soul."

45

"Georgianne talks about her mother now and again. She sounds like she was a wonderful woman."

I nodded, a lump forming in my throat as it did every time the woman and her tragic accident came to mind. "I miss her very much."

"If this is the real you, Isabel, then know that *I* like you. Very much."

I drew my lower lip between my teeth. Could I declare how I felt? It was all happening so fast. My head was spinning. "I like you too."

I felt as the air was sucked from the room making it impossible to breathe. I waited for some sort of response, but he let the declaration sit there in the air between us.

The waiter returned, setting out plates in front of us. Only seconds passed before we were again alone, but it felt like long minutes.

"I dreaded coming to Montgomery, because I knew the news I had to deliver would devastate Layton, but you have been such a pleasant surprise. I'm grateful for this time to get to know you."

"I feel the same way. I have wondered what Layton's family was like."

"Have I lived up to the expectation? Layton sets a pretty high bar."

His comment surprised me. Not only because it was the first I'd seen of some tension between the two, but because— in my mind—Quinton had more notoriety. "If that is true, you've had no trouble leaping over it."

His eyes lit up again. "You are too kind. While I was rehearsing *Giselle*, my younger brother was lobbying nations for stronger child labor laws."

"Is it a competition? Both are notable accomplishments."

"It shouldn't be, but comparisons happen often between the two of us."

"I didn't mean to do that."

"Oh, I know. Maybe it comes from being in a large family. I find myself fighting to stand out."

"Do you sometimes wish you didn't have as many siblings as you do?"

He didn't hesitate. "I absolutely love the large family I was raised in."

Realizing how the question must have sounded, I tried to explain myself. "Obviously, you love your family. I didn't mean for you to pick siblings to get rid of. It's just unusual—these days—for families to be so large."

"I know many believe my parents went overboard—especially since Ronaria is a small country with limited resources."

"Are they criticized for that?"

"Sometimes. It is something I don't understand. How am I supposed to wish away one of my brothers or sisters? But, I do understand the concerns. It is something I think about."

"You want to have a smaller family?"

"I don't have a crystal ball that predicts the future, but when I envision my life five or ten years down the road, I don't see kids at all." He paused and picked up a piece of calamari from his plate. He took a bite and thoroughly chewed the food. "Layton has such a way with children. They instantly love him. Even Delilah, who had a chip on her shoulder the size of Ronaria, warmed up to him quickly. I don't have that natural magnetism around kids."

"How do *you* feel about *children*?"

"I have nothing against them, if that's what you mean. I just don't see myself as a parent. It is not the way I want to make my mark on the world."

I shifted my weight in the chair. Just when it seemed like we were connecting, I discovered this chasm between us. One I was not sure there was any way for us to cross.

All I could think about these past weeks was growing a family, and he had no desire to have even one child. "Most people think of children as leaving their mark—their legacy. How do you want to effect change? In the arts?"

The ease in his manner and posture I'd only seen brief glimpses of faded. He sat a little straighter, and the light in his eyes dimmed. "You don't think that is a valuable contribution to the world?"

"I didn't say that." I'd offended him. It was obvious in his mannerisms and tone. I wanted to take back my sharp reply, but I couldn't. "You know I think music, dance, and art make this world a more tolerable place to live."

He dipped his chin toward his chest. "I must apologize. I'm used to being judged harshly by my choice."

My stomach twisted. I hadn't meant to seem critical. Goodness knows I'd been in those shoes. I was just disappointed to learn we had such a different life view.

One time in particular came to mind. I'd been fourteen and in the current foster home for a couple of months. Even though they'd been patient at first—obviously warned about my difficult situation and hard outer shell—they'd become obsessed with my low grades. The harder they worked with me—no matter how compassionately—the more obstinate I'd become.

I couldn't see they tried to help me. In my confused state —I saw their actions as an attempt to mold me into something different, better. So, with some of the seedier element I'd become friends with at school, I began shoplifting.

Once caught, the final rejection I'd expected was delivered, and I was returned to the system.

"If you truly believe you are not meant to be a parent, I think it is good that you recognize that now, instead of after you start a family."

He met my gaze and wordlessly studied my face. A move I

was well familiar with by now. I felt like he was trying to read my reaction. After a moment, he spoke. "I can't even imagine how difficult your life was because of your mother's addictions."

My mother was not where I wanted this conversation to go, so I changed the subject back to Quinton. "What about marriage? Is that something you don't see yourself doing?"

"Do I look like a playboy?"

I wondered if he could take a bit of teasing and decided to test the waters. "Maybe a little, on the surface."

He shook his head, telling me he knew I was picking on him. "I very much like the idea of sharing my life with someone, but when you are part of a royal family, it is difficult to gauge if a person is truly interested in you and not a title."

"I've heard Layton say the same thing."

"But Layton found his match, so I hold out hope. How about you, Isabel? Do you see yourself living alone?"

I bristled. He'd given me an opening to tell him about my plans to adopt, and I knew I should be just as forthright as he'd been with me. If things did develop between us, he'd learn I'd kept this from him, it would be as if I lied.

But where was this going to go?

He was a prince, and I was a barista. We lived thousands of miles away. I wanted a family of my own, and he didn't. He might flirt with me—tease me a little—but soon he would return to Ronaria.

We'd probably never see each other again.

There was no harm in continuing to keep my plans to adopt to myself, especially since I wanted Georgianne to hear about it from me. "I would welcome companionship, but there isn't anyone breaking down my door."

"You said that before. I still find it hard to believe. You're a beautiful and kind woman. The right man will come along."

After we finished dinner, Quinton insisted we have

dessert. When I tried to rebuff, claiming I was stuffed, he ordered one scoop of pistachio ice cream and two spoons.

I couldn't help but think his insistence didn't read true with what Georgianne had said about his distaste toward sweet treats. Maybe it was an excuse to keep talking, because he only had one or two bites of the ice cream, leaving the rest to me while he sipped coffee. Our conversation flowed freely.

The longer we talked, the harder I found myself falling for him.

He listened to me—really cared about what I had to say— evidenced by the fact he asked insightful and poignant questions about my past and my current life.

His told me several stories about his years as a ballet dancer. Despite insisting he'd left that world behind and moved back to Ronaria on his own accord, it became evident he not only missed it but longed to perform again. When I brought it up again, however, he denied the desires.

After we finished dessert, he walked me back to my apartment.

When we were about halfway, he reached out and took my hand.

The motioned surprised—but also thrilled—me. Coupled with the stories we'd shared, my lust-filled fantasies were being melded to a feeling of closeness I'd never felt with any other man.

I stopped in front of the entrance leading to my second-floor apartment and waited for Quinton to say goodnight.

Instead he leaned back against the green wooden door and pulled me closer to him. His free hand coming to rest on my hip. "I have so enjoyed your company. I am not ready for this evening to end."

Even though his words could be construed as forward, I

knew how he felt. I felt the same way. "I have to be at the restaurant early to bake."

His gaze dropped. "I understand. Is there anything you need me to do for you?"

His actions this morning proved the kitchen or the running of a restaurant wasn't in his wheelhouse. It didn't stop me from wanting to see him. "If you want to come by early, I will make you breakfast before you go to the castle."

"I would like that. I may even be tempted enough to try one of your sweet treats."

If there had been any doubt left that he wanted to continue to see *me*, he'd just erased it. The truth was, he hadn't even left yet and I already ached for the next time we could be together. "If you come, I will make a quiche for you."

"I didn't know that was on Georgianne's menu."

"Only on special occasions. It is *my* specialty."

His mouth tipped, and his voice dipped to a soft, sultry tone. "What is so special about tomorrow?"

"You will be there."

"I will." He brought the hand he still held to his mouth and gently kissed my fingertips. "Until tomorrow, my sweet Isabel."

The voice inside begged for me to invite Quinton upstairs. But, to what end? As much as I loved his company and wanted to taste him, he would be leaving soon.

Though the chances of him ever taking the throne were as slight as Layton's—four brothers sat in line before him— Quinton seemed to embrace royalty much more seriously than Layton.

He might find himself entertained by me, but he would never enter a serious relationship with a woman whose past was a troubled as mine.

It didn't stop me from longing to know what it was like to kiss him.

I should live in this moment.

His comment about not wanting to leave made it obvious he had a similar yearning. I inched closer to him, filling the polite void he'd left. As I did, his hand slipped over my hip to the center of my back.

My mouth hovered just below his, waiting for some indication he wanted it as much as I did. Or maybe I wanted him to save me from myself—stop me from the inevitable embarrassment.

"What do you want, Isabel?"

"To kiss you."

"What stops you?"

Nothing. A small forward movement and our lips met. He let me take the lead, encouraging me with a circular caress to the small of my back. The fingertips of his other hand brushed against my cheek.

Timid at first, I kissed him gently, but with his encouragement, our passion grew. Quinton tightened his embrace, and deepened the kiss.

Breathless, I leaned back moments later. Quinton looked at me with a passion the warmed my flesh.

"I like the way you say goodnight."

"Is that what you want? To leave now."

He leaned in and brushed my lips with his own. "No. What I want to do is not proper given the short time we've known each other." He slid his fingers under my chin. "So, I think it best I leave, but I look forward to your quiche in the morning."

He turned from me and started walking up the street. I leaned against the painted wood, and watched him until he reached the end of the street and rounded the corner.

Never once did he look back. Did he even know I watched him?

What it must be like to have such confidence.

Mindlessly, I chewed on my thumbnail, enjoying the crisp night air and wondering if I'd done the right thing. The floating feeling in my stomach and my near giddiness eased my fears of stepping out of line.

I pulled the keys from my purse, unlocked the door, and climbed the steps to the apartment, counting the hours until I could see Quinton again.

CHAPTER SEVEN

I arrived at the restaurant early to begin the baking. It wasn't like I could sleep anyway. I'd spent a few hours tossing and turning, the memory of Quinton's lips on mine chasing away sleep.

What was I thinking taking things to the next level, when I knew we had such different feelings about the future.

I should have told him the truth about my plans to adopt.

I will tell him this morning.

It's the only thing that's fair.

After finishing the baking, I made the quiche I promised Quinton for breakfast and took special care to set the table. I was filling the water glasses when I saw the car Montgomery's royal family had loaned Quinton pull up in front of the bistro.

A driver got out and held the door for him.

I watched Quinton talk to the man for a moment. He stood with his pelvis tipped and his feet in first position—a consummate dancer with a mix of royalty—while he buttoned his suit jacket. As he turned and headed toward the door, the driver got back in the car and drove away.

The castle was within walking distance, so I surmised that was his plan.

I set the pitcher on the table, crossed the dining room, unlocked the door, and held it for him. "Good morning," I greeted before making sure the door was locked again.

As I turned back to face him, he swept me into his arms and kissed me, laying me over his arm. I submitted to him, accepting his advances and snaking my arms over his shoulders.

He took his time. With each moment that passed and each caress to my flesh, my yearning for him increased.

Breaking the kiss a moment later, he slipped back a step.

I placed my hands on his chest and mimicked what he said last night. "I like the way you say hello."

He laughed and fingered a strand of my hair that had fallen loose of its confines. "I've thought of nothing else for the past seven hours and forty-five minutes."

"Are you sure about the timing?" I tried to joke, even though my nerves had my hands trembling.

"Quite certain." His posture was perfect, but I could tell he was nervous too by the way his mouth twitched. "I've barely slept. All I could think about all night was the way you caught my eye from the moment I walked into this place. I've become addicted to your smile and find myself saying things just so you honor me by flashing another one. And then you kissed me."

I watched his Adam's apple bob as he swallowed hard. It would seem he was as affected as I was by the intimacy. "You enjoyed it?"

His eyes twinkled. "Yes." He rubbed the back of his neck. "Maybe I'm crazy, but I've moved my schedule around so I can spend a lot of time here over the next month or so. I'm hoping you would be interested in taking the time to get to know each other better."

Equal amounts of thrill and fear coursed my veins. My heart raced. Maybe *my* prince *had* danced into my life. "I'd like that. But, are you sure you can?"

"I cannot take a full month off, but I do have some flexibility. I can get a lot of my work done over the phone and video conference calls. For you, I'm willing to make an effort."

If we were going to attempt a relationship, though, I had to be honest and tell him about my plans, but I shouldn't do it in a rush. I grabbed his hand and led him toward the table I'd arranged. "Come and sit. You should eat before it gets cold. I'm sure you're expected at the castle."

He took his seat and motioned for me to join him. "Actually, no. I am at your disposal until I meet my family's plane with the children at the airport."

Maybe I had time to tell him now. "When will it be in?"

"I expect them around eight."

Plenty of time. I checked my watch, and my heart sank. "I have to open the doors in twenty minutes. Let me get your espresso."

"That is not—" I swept away, rounding the long counter and working the large stainless-steel machine. Thank heavens I had set it up and all I had to do was push start.

My hands shook. I'd wanted Quinton's declaration as much as I'd wanted the new life I'd been planning, but could the two live in harmony?

"Isabel!" His voice echoed across the empty dining room. "We have such short time before I must share you with customers. I do not need the espresso, but I do want to spend a few moments with you."

I returned to the table, setting the small white cup on the table in front of him. After sitting, I sliced a piece of the quiche and placed it on his plate. "Have you heard from Layton and Georgianne?"

56

He took a bite of the egg dish. The expression on his face told me he liked it before he said the words. "Georgianne needs to make this a regular on the menu. It is absolutely fantastic."

Somehow his compliment meant more than any I'd received. "You will have to tell her that."

"Don't think I won't. And, yes, I spoke with Layton briefly last night. Seeing Delilah in her current state has him unnerved. The doctor did several tests yesterday and hoped to have all the results this morning. Layton was trying to stay positive, but I know he is anxious to hear the report."

"Please, send that poor child my love. Will Layton call you after the meeting?"

"I asked him too."

"I thought Georgianne would call for the sales reports. I know she worries about her business, even though we've been doing well for a while now."

"Layton and Delilah are her focus right now."

"As they should be."

"My family tells me Layton is leaning on her heavily. It's a blessing she has you here. She's told me more than once she trusts you to handle things as she would." He turned his attention to his food, taking another bite and then sipping his espresso. "I wish there was some way you could come with me to greet the children."

I sipped from my juice and pushed the food around my plate. "I don't see how I can."

He reached across the table and patted my hand. "I know. You are required here. I can only imagine how upset the kids are, and while some of their caregivers are accompanying them, you have a gentle and kind way I know would make them feel welcome."

His description of me warmed my heart, but it was the way he worried for the kid's wellbeing that gave me a glimmer of hope. Maybe my desires to adopt wouldn't be a deal breaker for us. "For someone who claims to not understand children, you have a good grasp of what they are going through."

"I empathize with their situation. It doesn't mean I'm capable of giving them the emotional support they need."

His words doused the flame of hope, and I chastised myself for even thinking it. How naive to think I could mold someone else, especially someone as confident and self-aware as Quinton.

I needed to tell him about my plans.

Now.

Delaying it would only make the situation more complicated, but it wasn't something I could do in the ten minutes left before I opened the doors.

Later.

I stood and began collecting my dishes. "My crew will be arriving any minute. I need to do the final prep work. Where are the children going once you've picked them up at the airport?"

"The orphanage."

It would be a chaotic scene. We wouldn't be able to talk then, but tonight.

Definitely tonight.

"I will bring over lunches for the children and staff—some soup and sandwiches—around eleven. I won't have a lot of time. I can't leave Marcus and the ladies alone during the rush."

Quinton stood and picked up his own plate. "But you will stay and eat with me."

"I don't know."

His fingers pinched my chin. He pleaded with his eyes. "Yes. You do."

I couldn't deny him, so I simply nodded.

*W*e'd been extremely busy from the moment I opened the doors. Quinton jumped in and helped in any way he could, despite the fact he was out of his element.

He bused tables, made drinks, served food, and packaged takeout orders. When his car arrived, he'd sought me out in the kitchen where I was trying to help the cooks catch up with orders.

He pulled me aside and kissed me gently. "I'll see you soon?"

I nodded and tried to push aside my guilt for not telling him the truth last night.

The longer I waited the more complicated it became. With every longing stare he gave me, each touch of his hand, and each soft kiss, I felt myself falling more and more under his spell.

And the root of my guilt took deeper hold.

Now, the kitchen staff bustled around me as I tried to focus on the activity of packaging lunches for the displaced children and staff from the Italian orphanage. Quinton had called to let me know all the children and chaperones would be staying in Montgomery until this evening. They'd kept their pilot so busy over the last few days, he was required to rest. Quinton reported James's staff was so overwhelmed by the influx of people, they were grateful I'd offered to bring food.

Marcus helped me load the boxes in my car, and while I drove the short distance to the orphanage, I couldn't stop wondering how Quinton would react when I told him my truth.

When I'd kissed him last night, I was willing to accept a

fleeting moment in time with him—a few days of exploring the physical attraction.

I believed we were too different to be have anything more than a brief affair.

Then I'd seen the hunger in his eyes before he'd initiated the passion-filled kiss this morning. He heard me talk about my turbulent past and still rearranged his schedule so we could explore the *developing feelings.*

He saw something more than a physical spark.

If I were honest with myself, I'd seen it too. Now, I feared the information I'd held back last night would unravel it all.

At the orphanage, I stacked the two boxes of food and picked them up. I'd have to come back for the milk and juice.

Mrs. Tillie met me at the door, opening it for me and then taking the top box. "Let me help you with that, dear. It was so kind of you to do this."

I followed the woman down the hall, uncomfortable with the woman's praise. If I was as kind as they made me out to be, wouldn't I have been honest with Quinton before I'd indicated I was interested in a relationship, especially since he'd been honest with me about his insecurities. And what about my desires. If I really wanted to adopt, why had I struggled to pick a child and move forward with my foster parent training? "I know it is what Georgianne would do if she were here."

"You're right about that. However, I know this cause is important to you too, dear." She leaned her hip against the bar handle pushing the door to the recreation room open.

It was like a large gymnasium, with basketball hoops on either side of the room. Instead of a wood floor, however, there was a cream-colored linoleum. The lines of a basketball court—as well as a few other games—were painted on the floor in different colors.

The room was an add-on since the days I lived here. It

had only been built in the last year, thanks to fundraising Layton had headed.

Three eight-foot tables had been set up in the center of the room, and the kids and adults were seated at them.

I didn't immediately see Quinton and wondered where he could be. Then I heard his voice behind me.

I set the food on the table and then spun on my heel to see him crossing to me, still talking on his cell phone. When he got close, he said goodbye, disconnected the phone, and slipped into the pocket of his suit jacket before greeting me with a chaste kiss to my cheek. "Thank you so much."

"I still have drinks in the car, let me go grab them."

Winifred jumped back up. "Let me. Is your car unlocked?"

I nodded but quickly gave my attention back to Quinton. It was evident in his eyes something laid heavy on his mind.

Before I could ask what, he took my elbow and guided me away from the crowd. "That was Layton on the phone."

"How is Delilah?"

"She's doing well, I guess. Honestly, I'm quite concerned. The doctor has told her, Layton, and Georgianne he can operate on the tumor. Everyone is excited, but I'm skeptical."

"Why? You called *this* doctor because you hoped he could do what the others claimed they couldn't."

He nodded, but his face was solemn. "He wants to operate immediately. The sooner the better."

"What does Delilah want?"

"To move forward, of course. She wants to live. Layton agrees. They will be starting the surgery within the hour."

"You are worried about the risks?"

"It's her brain. Of course, there are risks." He spat the words from his mouth, their sharp edge cutting at me.

"From what you said, if they do nothing, she will die. There is no question of that, right?"

"You are correct, but why do they have to move so

61

quickly? Shouldn't they take the time to weigh the benefits and the risks?"

"The way I see it, if it's successful she gets her life back."

"And if this doctor is an egotistical fool who believes he is God, she might die on the table."

"She's going to die anyway."

He clenched his hands at his side and then covered his mouth with one of them. I was sure I'd heard him curse beneath his breath, but he made every effort to hide it. I thought it best not to draw attention to his slip.

Instead I stepped closer and reached out to hug him.

He threw up his arms defensively, blocking my embrace. "I'm sorry. I just… This isn't the time."

I stepped back, crossing my arms. "No, my apologies. I only meant to comfort you."

He dipped his chin and pushed a hand through his hair. "This is too much to deal with. I hate that I'm so far away. Delilah and my brother—all of our family—need me, and I'm here." His gaze flickered back to the table. I followed his stare and saw the agency's staff passing out the food and the drinks. "I should go help."

"Quinton. If you want to go back to Ronaria, you should. James and Queen Margaret can manage the orphans. I can manage the restaurant."

His shoulders slumped, and his chest deflated. "So there is no reason for me to stay?"

He didn't wait for my response, only walked toward the table and began pitching in. He helped the children unwrap the sandwiches and opened the bottles of juice. His own misery seemed to evaporate as he spoke kindly to the children, giving his best attempts to make them laugh.

Sometimes it took more than one attempt, but he didn't move on to the next child until he completed the mission.

I watched him. It was obvious Quinton adored children and—just like his younger brother—had a way with them.

Why then was he so insistent on not becoming a father?

And why was he so angry with me? Had he somehow found out about my plans?

CHAPTER EIGHT

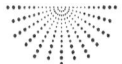

For the next hour, I helped with the children. I waited for Quinton to come back and ask me to eat with him or explain why he'd pushed me away when I tried to hug him. Instead he continued to work—barely looking up at me.

On occasion, when he thought no one was watching, I would see him step away from the crowd and check his phone.

I needed to get back to the restaurant and contemplated saying goodbye, but decided he needed some time to himself.

Time to think.

He knew where I was if he needed me.

When I arrived at the diner, we were deep into the lunch rush. I immediately jumped into the mix and helped take care of the customers. I hardly had time to think about Quinton, until I caught a glimpse of him coming through the door.

A glance at the clock told me it was nearly three. How long had it taken him to realize I'd left?

I bit my tongue and felt guilty for being bitter. I couldn't even be sure his bad temper had been directed at me. Like everyone, he was worried sick about Delilah.

After taking the customer's order, I headed back to the counter. As I passed him, he reached out for my elbow, but I stepped to the side. "Just a moment."

His face was solemn as he hopped up on a stool and waited for me to punch the order into the point of sale machine.

From the corner of my eye I saw Jana making Quinton an espresso and took a moment to collect myself. As unfair as it was to hold his reaction against him, it had hurt me. Adding my emotion to an already tumultuous pot could only make matters worse.

I took a deep breath and paced back to the counter.

When I was close, he pushed his fingers through his hair. "I owe you an apology."

Though he seemed frazzled, his voice was devoid of regret. In fact, I heard no emotion behind his words at all, almost as if he was shutting down.

Stomach acid bubbled up as my anger turned to guilt. "It's been a rough day."

"I need to talk to you, and I don't want to do it here. Can you leave? We can go to Layton's."

"I'm still on the clock."

He closed his eyes and gripped the counter. "Please. I can't have this discussion in public."

I looked around the dining room it was nearly empty. Myra would be here in less than an hour. "Okay." I turned to Jana. "Will you be all right if I leave a little early."

"Sure, honey. I have it under control."

"Tell Myra I will call her after a bit to check in." I then turned back to Quinton. "Do you want me to meet you at Georgianne and Layton's?"

"That would probably be best." Quinton fidgeted on the

stool for a moment. He looked as if he might reach out and touch my hand, but instead he changed his mind, got up, and left.

He waited for the driver to open the door to the car before sliding in. I let Jana—and then the kitchen staff—know they could call me if they needed anything and left the diner.

On the short drive, my mind went in a thousand different directions. Something had shifted in Quinton from the time he left me in the morning and when I'd seen him again a couple hours later. Though Delilah's surgery was enough to cause that much worry, I got the feeling it was about so much more.

The only thing that made sense was he'd heard about my intentions to adopt, but who would have told him, and why would it matter? The only commitment we'd made was to test the sparks flying between us to see if a sustainable flame was possible.

I parked the car on the street in front of their Victorian home and quickly walked up the walk. Before I could knock on the door, Quinton was holding it open for me. In the foyer, I noticed his bags packed and sitting at the bottom of the steps.

He followed my gaze and answered my unasked question. "I'm flying back to Ronaria tonight, with the displaced children."

A million questions raced through my mind all at once, but I couldn't find the way to ask any of them. "I see."

He leveled his gaze. It was hard and icy, like I'd seen it when he was on the phone the first day in the bistro.

"What did I do?"

He swallowed hard, and I saw a chink in his armor. He was using anger as a mask for his pain. "It's more about what you didn't say."

He *had* heard the truth. But not from me. "How did you…" It didn't matter. "I was going to tell you, Quinton. I tried to last night, but we were having such a nice time. At the moment, I thought we were keeping it casual."

"And then you kissed me. I took that to mean you wanted more."

"I did. I do."

"You are in the process of adopting a child! Maybe you are right to say I didn't need to know that *before* the moment you kissed me. But, you knew how I felt. And you knew how much I detest having my time wasted."

Really? His irritation wasn't about our different goals, but because I had wasted his precious time? "I was going to tell you."

"When? This morning, when I told you I had cleared my schedule for the next month, might have been a good time."

"I wanted to."

"But you didn't. And then at lunch?"

"You wouldn't even look at me."

"Because I'd just found out you lied to me."

I crossed my arms and leaned back against the door. "I should have told you, but I didn't lie."

His body sagged, and he shifted his weight. "I want to believe you wouldn't have kept this secret for long."

"I swear it."

"Would you be willing to put off adoption for a time?" There was a desperation in his voice. He was asking me to give up something I held very dear. Of course, he didn't know just how much I wanted it, because we hadn't yet had the discussion.

"How long?"

He shrugged. "How about for the month I originally cleared for us to explore a relationship."

Thirty days. Just a blip of time in the grand scheme of

things, but would it be time simply wasted. "Do you think you might change *your* mind?"

He covered his mouth with a closed fist. His stare never left my face, but I felt like he was examining himself more than me. "It's funny. I've been asking myself the same question since I overhead James scheduling your home study with the social worker. I've been racking my mind trying to come up with some way we can bridge this gap between us, because—damn it, Isabel—I want you!"

It should have been one of the happiest moments of my life. He was here, interested in me, and willing to do the work to see if we could build a future. But he was asking me to make a choice—to give up something I'd longed for.

I rubbed my temples. "A family. It's the one thing I've known—with all my heart—I've wanted. If you're asking me to put it on hold until we explore these feelings between us. Yes. I can absolutely give this some time. But, I don't want to put off having a family forever."

"Are you asking me if my mind is set, or if I may someday want children of my own?" He shook his head. "My work requires me to travel, and I don't feel like I'm ready for such a commitment."

I took a step closer to Quinton. Even though I believed this was probably the last time we'd talk like this, I couldn't resist my urge to touch him—kiss him—again. The memory of him pushing me away held me back, waited for him to signal me it was all right."

He met me in the middle, taking a step too. He held out his hand, and I accepted the gesture, squeezing his fingers.

"Let's go sit. I feel like I need to explain myself."

He led me down the small hall into the open-air family room. My attention was immediately drawn to the paintings Quinton had proudly showed me the first morning we met in the bistro. "They're perfect."

He admired the paintings for a moment and nodded his appreciation. "I'm quite pleased with the way they look in this room."

We sat together on the small loveseat. He cradled my hand in both of his before placing them on his lap.

"I don't want you to misconstrue anything I say. I love my family, and I am grateful for the way I was raised. I have missed my brother over the last eighteen months. His visits are never long enough and are a poor substitute for the closeness we once shared."

"I understand, probably more than you know." As hard as I tried to lock up my emotions, I could feel tears glossing my eyes. I couldn't reconcile how he felt this way, yet felt so strongly about having a family of his own.

"Ronaria is small. Our resources are few. Most of our citizens work very hard in manufacturing jobs and farming. They struggle to make ends meet. The average couple has one child. A family of four is considered large. Yet, my parents had seven boys and three girls."

"They have the means to care for all of you."

He nodded curtly. "And my father, Garett, and Brennan work tirelessly to bring more work to our nation. Broderick and Adrian are focused on working with other nations—like Montgomery—to bring opportunities to our people and improve living conditions."

"Your work hard too. Your work is important."

He met my gaze. For an ever-so-brief moment, a smile replaced his somberness. "I've tried to bring art programs into our education system. I've known of the need long before you told me the story about your dance classes, but I am blocked by members of my own family who say we must improve living conditions before we enhance their lives. Before he came to work with Margaret, I was told to leave the care of our nation's children to Layton."

"I don't understand. Why can't the two of you work together on the issue?"

"Layton does well on the world stage. My father appreciates his ability to foster relationships with other nations." He paused and scratched at his chin. "I must be sounding like an insufferable brat. I don't mean that. I'm very proud of all my brother does."

"I can tell." My heart ached for him. It was becoming evident to me he felt he was lost in the crowd—despite the fact he'd been a celebrity just a few short years before.

"When Layton decided to take the job with the foundation, and Father—based on Layton's recommendation—put Aunt Alma in his place, she needed help, understandably. There was a lot to learn, and I was eager to assist. It's been, as you said, the opportunity to take my work with the arts to a new level. I've brought programs to our foster care system *and* our schools."

He had the power to do the things I wanted to, but couldn't. If adopting had been his goal, he was the kind of person who would move forward, not agonize over every detail like I had. "I think that's amazing."

"You would be so interested in the results we've seen, but that is another story. I'm trying to stay on track." He paused and swallowed. "These are hard things for me to say."

The angst I had seen at the agency this morning was back, the façade he normally kept in place of being in control was crumbling. I knew he didn't show everyone this side, and I wanted to honor the fact he felt he could be himself with me. I scooted my body closer and laid my free hand on top of his. "You can tell me, and no matter what happens, it will stay with me."

My words seemed to give him a boost of confidence, something I never believed he had in short supply. "Even though I have been there with Delilah from the moment she started getting sick until I left to come get Layton for her, he didn't even consult me on the big decision." He shook his head, and looked away. "I don't mean to make this about me. It's not about the decision—I want the best for Delilah. I'm worried sick about her."

"I know. We all are." I paused, gave him a few seconds to continue explaining but could see the struggle was tearing him apart. "Is it more about feeling like no matter how hard you work, what good you do, you get lost in the shuffle of your large family?"

He leaned back on the couch. His shoulders relaxed as if he'd been able to drop a heavy weight. "In part. A big part. But also, people of our country hold an opinion. Instead of the arts, they think I should focus on economic issues. They don't understand how it can improve their lives—and the lives of the next generation. They can't wrap their minds around the facts and the statistics of how a child who is taught music and dance becomes better at math and cognitive learning. They don't make the connection to how these skills will help him in the work force. They want their children to have reliable jobs that pay well. They don't want them to hang their hats on being a dancer like I was before Father called me home."

"You resent giving up dancing?"

He took a deep breath. "I already told you I do not."

The pained lines on his face told me it wasn't black and white for him. "I never gave it up. The dancer still lives in here." He used our entwined hands to tap on his chest. "And I feel good using what I know to help others, but I cannot stop now. I still have work to do. I will not bring children into this world—or into my family—while I am still travelling and working. If the time ever comes that I do have children, they will never feel like just *another* child in a large home." He paused and took a deep breath. I felt his hand tremble and watched his eye twitch. Whatever he had to say, he feared asking. "We are so very young. I can't promise you we will be able to build a relationship that will last forever, but I'm asking you to give us just a little time to sort it out."

I slipped my hands from his clutch and stood. I walked across the room and looked at the painting that now hung over the fireplace. The bright blues I'd interpreted as cold— symbolic of the weather—I now saw differently. I saw desolation and loneliness, but also hope. I spun back to Quinton. "Having a family all my own is something I've longed for since the day my mother allowed me to be ripped away."

He dropped his gaze to the floor. "I ask too much of you."

Quickly, I closed the distance between us. "No. you don't. Let me finish. For you—for a chance to be us—I can wait a little longer."

He stood and pulled me into his arms. His lips brushed mine—tentatively at first—but when I laid my arms over his shoulders and pushed up on my toes to kiss him again, he deepened the affection.

After our kiss came to a natural end, he still held me close. "We may be setting ourselves up for more pain. If these blossoming feelings take deep roots, our different feelings about family are no small obstacle to overcome."

I nodded. "A week ago, moving forward with an adoption had been all I could think about. I started this process with the agency without a particular child in mind."

"I don't think that is so unusual. You planned to begin by fostering, yes?"

"I did. But since we met, I began to...not doubt my decisions, but question them. I tried to say it was because Georgianne might close *Viviana's Bistro* to move to Ronaria. I began to fear my abilities to care for a child."

"Again, I think these are normal fears when faced with such a big decision."

"Maybe. Regardless, I'm okay with taking a few weeks to sort out my fears and these feelings for you." I was beginning to see in Quinton's eyes and feel in his embrace a new version of the family I'd ached for. For the first time I was beginning to understand it wasn't James, Viviana, or Georgianne who had put caveats on their relationship with me. Those were definitions and stipulations I had created. The same was true with the many foster families I'd been too wounded by or too afraid to trust in.

If things worked out with Quinton, maybe my family would be the two of us. To my surprise, the thought didn't make my heart ache as the idea of being alone had just a few days ago.

He kissed my forehead. "I'm sorry I went a little crazy today."

I laid my hand against his cheek. "I don't blame you. I should have been more honest."

His phone rang, and I slipped from his arms. We both knew it must be Layton or someone with word about Delilah.

He stared at the caller ID for a brief second before answering. "How is she, Layton?"

I watched waves of relief roll through him, and he took a sharp inhale.

"I'm so pleased. So very happy...of course. Of course." He pinched the bridge of his nose. "No. I'm sending the plane with the children and chaperones this evening, but I'm going to stay on in Montgomery a while longer." He squeezed my hand and gave me a look of question as he spoke. "When Delilah is well enough for visitors, I will be there to see her."

I gave him a nod of support, as I found myself falling a little harder for the man in front of me.

CHAPTER NINE

I stood in front of Georgianne's stove putting the final touches on the dinner I'd prepared. Over the last six weeks, I'd become quite comfortable maneuvering their kitchen while fixing the occasional dinner for Quinton.

The deadline on the month-long trial period had come and gone, and we continued to spend as much time together as possible.

Layton had stayed in Ronaria throughout Delilah's recovery, and while Georgianne had come home twice, for three days each time, she'd quickly returned to her fiancé's side after the short visits with her father and me.

It'd been two days since Quinton had flown to Ronaria for meetings with his father. Now, Georgianne and the brothers were coming back for the foreseeable future—with Delilah.

I knew this was a turning point for Quinton. His father expected him to return to Ronaria, and he'd planned to have what I knew would be difficult discussions with the king. When I asked him about the details, he said he preferred to wait until solid plans had been formed.

I heard a scuffle at the front door and then Georgianne's voice filtered down the hallway. "We're home!"

Home.

Was this really going to be their home base?

Somehow the fear she'd close the bistro had eased. James's and Quinton's words had sunk in. I knew whatever choices Georgianne made, I was strong enough and self-sufficient. I would maneuver them and move forward.

"In here," I called out. "I hope everyone is hungry."

Georgianne entered the kitchen, Layton was a few steps behind her walking side by side with Delilah who looked well and was moving on her own, albeit at a slow pace.

Georgianne came straight to me, wrapping me in an embrace. "I've missed you." She whispered in my ear before pulling back and looking over the pots and pans. "You went to so much trouble. Everything smells delicious."

"It was no trouble." I met Quinton's gaze. "I wanted to welcome you home."

"We appreciate it very much." Layton held a chair for Delilah, before coming to greet me with a hug as Georgianne had.

I returned Layton's embrace, meeting Delilah's gaze over his shoulder. "Can I get you anything, honey."

She shook her head and seemed to concentrate before speaking. "I'm good." The teen looked to Georgianne. "A little tired."

"It was a long flight. Would you rather lie down for now?"

"Yes. Please."

Georgianne rounded the table and motioned to Layton. "Let's get her settled in the guest room." She looked over her shoulder and met Quinton's gaze. "I think Quinton missed you, Isabel."

I didn't know how to answer that. He'd only been gone a

couple of days, but I hungered to touch him. "I'll get lunch on the table."

Quinton hung back, leaned against the door jamb, only moving when Delilah, Georgianne, and Layton neared the doorway.

When we were alone, he closed the distance. I laid my arms on his shoulders and pushed up on my toes to welcome him back with a kiss.

"I missed you," he whispered against my lips.

"It feels like it's been weeks instead of days."

He gripped my hand and brought it to his mouth, kissing my knuckles. "I'm ready to have that talk you've been asking about. Can we go in the other room?"

I turned off the stove's burners and followed him into the living room. We sat next to each other on the couch as we had six weeks earlier. Back then, I'd been twisted up in knots because we stood at a cross road. Now I felt at ease, knowing we'd be able to figure out what the future held.

"I would like you to come back to Ronaria with me."

His words knocked the wind from my chest. He'd made it very clear he'd have to return one day soon, but because he'd put it off this long, it seemed like it still lingered in the distance. That it was something we didn't have to think about right now.

My surprise must have been evident, because he laid a hand on my cheek. "Deep breath."

I leaned into his touch and followed his direction. My eyes drifted closed.

"Another," he directed.

Again, I inhaled slow and deep, giggling because he'd remembered the trick I told him James always used to calm me down.

"Don't think about the logistics. What does your heart say? Would you consider it?"

When I hushed the noise of my mind and listened only to my heart, there was only one choice. "Yes. If you need to go back, I will go with you."

"Now that Layton is here, I must return to my home base and my work." He paused and a smile lit up his whole face.

I knew in an instant his hope—his dream—had come to be. "Your father approved the ballet?"

"Yes. The Slovakian ballet will be coming to perform in Ronaria in the fall, and I will be the principal dancer in the production. It will serve as a fundraiser to bring music and dance into our schools. I must begin rehearsals with the company in two weeks."

I threw my arms around his neck. "I'm so happy for you! How is it going to work? Will you go to Slovakia to prepare?"

"They are relocating to Ronaria, so I can tend to my other duties, but I must work with them religiously. I am out of shape, I fear."

I poked his ribs. "You are *not* out of shape. I've watched you work at it daily."

"True, but if I'm to be ready for this performance I will have to work much more than an hour a day. I will not be as available for you as I have been."

"It will be worth it for you to have this dream of yours." Still, I couldn't keep the questions and concerns quiet for long. They popped around in my head. Yes, I wanted to be there for Quinton, and I wouldn't miss his performance for the world. But what about Georgianne? "It might take time to work out the details before I could join you. I don't want to leave Georgianne in the lurch. She counts on me. Also, I would need to find work and a place to live in Ronaria."

He laid a finger against my lips. "It may have been presumptuous of me, but I know how you treasure your independence. I've made some inquires and have some leads."

My head tipped. It didn't surprise me he'd worked out all the details. It was his way. The Quinton I'd come to know so well. "What did you find?"

As if on cue, Georgianne came down the steps. "Did she say yes?"

Quinton chuckled. "Forgive me, but I did involve Georgianne."

My attention snapped to her. She looked so pleased with herself as she rounded the couch, touching Quinton's shoulder before taking a seat in the chair to my left. "I think the best place to start is that Layton and I have set a date— June eighteenth."

Today was the twenty-third of June. "Of next year, I assume."

She nodded. "We wanted sooner, but we also wanted something out of the public eye." She eyed Quinton and then turned her attention back to me. "Layton's parents persuaded us that choice was selfish. In order to have a proper wedding, we need a year to plan."

"I'm so excited."

"I am too. Exhausted already, but thrilled. This time spent in Ronaria has been eye-opening. I've seen first-hand the struggle and the poverty Layton and Quinton have told me about. When their mother appealed to me to begin considering a way I could work in service to the country's people, I knew instantly the cause I wanted to take on. The details are still sketchy, and I'm working with the king and queen to clarify the vision. I want to clone *Viviana's*, but in a way that we can help feed the hungry and homeless. We want to the sales from the business side to support the charity work."

"That's incredible."

"We want to move forward as soon as possible, and there is a lot of work to be done. Layton still has nine months in his contract with Margaret's foundation, but we plan to return to Ronaria next March. I need someone there I can count on to be my eyes and my ears. Even before I knew how close you and Quinton had grown, you were the first person I thought of—the only one I want."

"You would like me to go ahead to Ronaria and help open your new business."

"And the charity, yes. I will be travelling back and forth as much as possible, but I need someone on the ground who knows how I think and understands the way I run a business —my family."

Words escaped me. Even if knew *what* to say, a lump had formed in my throat, preventing the words. I nodded, blinking away the forming tears.

Georgianne had voiced what I'd come to learn over the last several weeks. My view of family had been skewed. What I'd longed for so desperately, I already had in James and Georgianne. It was now expanding to include Quinton.

I still had the desire to grow my family with children, but it wasn't as immediate as it had been before. I was willing to give Quinton the time he'd requested.

I found my feet and went to Georgianne. She stood to accept my hug. "Yes. I'll go."

She squeezed me tight. "Thank you. I can't tell you how much it means to me that you'll do this."

When she pulled back, her gaze flickered between Quinton and me. "Layton will be down any minute, he was making sure Delilah is comfortable. I'll leave you two to finish your conversation while I put the food on the table."

I turned back to face Quinton and found him directly in front of me. "I've been thinking about the conversation we had several weeks ago."

"Me too."

"Being with you has opened my eyes. I've been examining my life, my choices, and my goals." He paused. His chest inflated with a deep breath. "I love you, Isabel." He pushed his hand into the pocket inside his jacket and dropped to one knee.

When he offered up the platinum ring with a large emerald-cut diamond, I thought my heart had stopped beating.

"Isabel, as this day approached when I knew I would have to make plans to return home, my heart ached. I can't imagine my life without you. I want you with me. Need you by my side. I don't want to jump into having children, I want some time for the two of us. Knowing you has changed me. When I look in the future now, I *can* see a family. Would you please marry me?"

I wiped the tears of joy that strayed down my cheek. I encouraged him to stand, so I could hold him close. "Yes. Yes, I will marry you."

His eyes glossed over, and his hand trembled as he slid the ring on to my finger.

I encased his face in my hands and kissed him. "I want you to know I've done some self-examination over the last few weeks too. Being with you has made me rethink my definition of family. What I was searching for—a place where I belonged and people who loved me unconditionally—I already had. *You* will be my family and my home. I do hope we decide—together—to make our family larger. If you never become comfortable with the idea, I will be content with *you*."

He started at my temple slowly running his fingertips down the side of my face. He had no more words, but he never really needed them. He was able to convey every message he had through his eyes, his movements, and his touch.

I had no doubt. He loved me and trusted that I loved *him*.

The prince.

The dancer.

The man.

I closed my eyes and leaned into his touch.

He left a chaste kiss on my forehead. "Let's go eat the lunch you prepared. We must talk to our family and make plans." He slipped an arm around my waist and I curled my body to his.

No matter what the future held, I knew I could count on my ever-growing family to celebrate the joys and help me through the disappointments. When Georgianne needed me the most, I'd been strong enough to step up and be someone she could count on.

Now, she was raising the bar, giving me more responsibility.

With that faith and Quinton's love, I knew none of us would fail. We would always love each other and we'd always be a family.

ACKNOWLEDGMENTS

Thank you:

First and always to my family: Brad Phillips, Josh Phillips, Jessica Phillips, and Katelynn Phillips. Without your patience, understanding, and support, I would not be able to spend my time in my imaginary worlds.

To my *Crew*. In particular: Kathy Satterlee, Mary Kenton, Erika Mounts, and Sherry Halcomb. You amazing support is humbling.

To my editor: Gilly Wright. You Rock! Thank you hard work!

ABOUT CONSTANCE PHILLIPS

Constance Phillips lives in Ohio with her husband, daughter, and four canine kids where she writes contemporary romance novels and paranormal romance novels.

When not writing stories of finding and rediscovering love, Constance and her husband spend the hours planning a cross-country motorcycle trip for the not-so-distant future…if they can find a sidecar big enough for the pups.

Subscribe to my newsletter and get a copy of *Lexi's Choice* for free

CONNECT WITH CONSTANCE

You can find news and information about new releases,
appearances, signings, etc at the following places.

Newsletter: http://www.constancephillips.com/newsletter-signup.html
Website: http://www.constancephillips.com
Facebook: https://www.facebook.com/ConstancePhillipsromanceAuthor/
Twitter: https://www.twitter.com/CPhillips
Instagram: https://www.instagram.com/cmphillips1967/

MORE BOOKS BY CONSTANCE PHILLIPS

RONARIA'S PRINCES
Royal Holiday
Raising the Royal Barre

THE REALM'S SALVATION SERIES
Fairyproof
Council Courtship (Novella)
Chasing Power

SUNNYDALE DAYS SERIES
All That's Unspoken
All That's Unclaimed
All That's Unrealized
All That's Unforgiven
All That's Unforeseen

SUNNYDAE WEDDINGS
Nate and Hailey

TO PROTECT AND SERVE

Love Reclaimed

Lone Star Leave (novella prequel)

Novellas

One Lucky Night (Lexi's Chance)

Refused to Reign

SINGLE TITLE

Resurrecting Harry

The Ultimate Catch